Hattie and Henry

Sammy put the hat on a little table beside him. He tapped it with his magician's wand and put his hand inside. This was when he would usually lift Hattie out of the secret pocket. Hattie held her breath. What would Sammy do when he realized she wasn't in the hat?

Then Hattie stared in amazement. Sammy had lifted out a little gray-and-white kitten!

Best ♥ Friends

Hattie and Henry

Best·Friends

Hattie and Henry

by Jenny Dale

Illustrated by Susan Hellard

SCHOLASTIC INC.

New York   Toronto   London   Auckland   Sydney

Mexico City   New Delhi   Hong Kong   Buenos Aires

Special thanks to Narinder Dhami

ISBN 0-439-79120-0

12 11 10 9 8 7 6 5 4 3 2   6 7 8 9 10 11/0

Printed in the U.S.A.
First printing, March 2006

chapter one

"I *love* being a magician's rabbit," Hattie snuffled happily. "I'm the luckiest rabbit in the whole world!"

Hattie peeked out of her basket, her little pink nose twitching with excitement. She and her owner, Sammy Spells, were on the way to perform at a school fair. Hattie couldn't *wait*. Her favorite trick was hiding in the secret pocket of Sammy's big black hat, and then popping out. The audience always loved that!

"Here we are, Hattie," said Sammy,

smiling down at her. Hattie's basket was next to him on the front seat of the van.

Hattie could see out of the window as they drove through some tall gates. The school playing field was bustling with activity. There were concession stands and a Ferris wheel, as well as pony rides, face painting, and a puppet show. Flags

fluttered and colorful balloons bobbed in the breeze.

Sammy parked the van and began to unload his magic equipment. Hattie waited in her basket, hopping up and down impatiently. She watched as Sammy carried the boxes one by one into a big red-and-white-striped tent.

Finally, Sammy carried Hattie into the tent. Rows of empty chairs were in front of a stage with silver screens behind it. Sammy took Hattie behind the screens, put the basket on a table, and opened it. "Off you go," he said, grinning.

Hattie knew exactly what to do. Her eyes shining, she lolloped out of the basket and went right over to the big top hat at the other end of the table. The hat was a bit old, and it had a tear in the side, but Hattie didn't mind. It was her *magic* hat. She jumped inside and looked up at Sammy.

"Good girl," said Sammy, stroking her ears. "Wait there. The show will be starting very soon."

Hattie snuggled down inside the top hat as Sammy went off. She didn't have to get into the secret pocket until the show was ready to start. Hattie wriggled with delight. She was so lucky to be Sammy's special, magic rabbit!

"What's going on?" Henry the kitten mewed curiously. "Can I go and see?"

He pushed his head through the bars of the front-yard gate and peered at the school playing field. "There are a lot of people and I smell delicious smells!" His whiskers twitched as he sniffed the air.

"Henry, you *must* stay in our yard," meowed his mom. Gently, she nudged the little gray-and-white kitten away from the gate. "Go and play with your sisters."

Henry glanced at his four fluffy sisters. They were running around on the lawn, chasing butterflies. Then he looked back at the playing field. "But that looks *much* more exciting!" he mewed.

Henry lived with his mom and his sisters and the Watts family in a house next to the school. Henry was used to seeing all the children going to and from school. They always stopped to stroke him. But today wasn't an ordinary school day. Something even more exciting was going on!

"Come on, Mom," called Jamie Watts as he ran into the yard. "We'll be late."

"No, we won't," laughed Mrs. Watts, following him outside. "The fair just started."

Henry's little pointed ears pricked up.

So that's what was happening in the playing field. A fair! Purring loudly, he followed Jamie over to the gate.

"Mom, can I go on a pony ride?" asked Jamie. "And can I have a caramel apple and some cotton candy?"

"We'll see . . ." said Mrs. Watts.

Henry listened eagerly, his tail waving wildly from side to side. As soon as Jamie opened the gate, he scampered over.

"Henry!" Jamie bent down and scooped up the kitten. "Where are you going?"

"To the fair, of course," Henry purred.

"You can't come with us," Jamie chuckled as he tickled him under the chin. To Henry's dismay, Jamie took him back into the yard and gently plopped

the kitten down beside his mom. "See
you later, Henry," Jamie said with a wave.

Henry flopped down on the grass,
feeling very miserable. "It's not fair," he
mewed. "Why can't *I* go, too?"

chapter two

Henry watched glumly as Jamie and his mom set off across the field.

"Never mind, Henry," meowed his mom, licking his ear. "When you are bigger, you and your sisters will be going to exciting new homes. Then you'll be able to have lots of adventures."

"But I don't want to wait till then," Henry protested.

"Shh, it's time for a snooze," his mom yawned. She was curled up on the soft grass with her four other kittens snuggled beside her.

Henry cuddled down next to them. The sun felt warm on his thick fur, but Henry didn't feel sleepy. He stared across the yard. He could see the fair through the bars of the gate. More and more people were arriving every minute.

Henry glanced at his mom and sisters. They were all fast asleep. "I could just have a *quick* look at the fair," he mewed to himself. "I won't be very long. I'll be back before they wake up."

His heart thudding with excitement, Henry quietly got up. He padded over to the gate and squeezed underneath it.

"Yes!" Henry purred, giving himself a

quick lick to smooth his ruffled fur. "I'm going to the fair!"

He set off across the grass. He had to dodge between lots of legs, but no one noticed the little kitten.

Henry didn't know where to go first. It was all very confusing. Children shouted and laughed as they ran around. Some of them were holding balloons, and others had brightly colored paint on their faces.

Then Henry spotted a huge red-and-white-striped tent in the middle of the field. He pricked up his ears. He could hear children laughing and clapping inside. "Maybe Jamie's in there," he mewed. "And maybe some of my friends from the school are in there, too!"

Purring loudly, Henry trotted over to the tent and wriggled under the canvas.

Hattie was still waiting quietly in the top hat on the table behind the screens. Sammy's magic show had started. Hattie popped her head out of the hat to listen to the audience clapping and cheering. "Not long now," she told herself. Soon, Sammy would come behind the screen, pick up the top hat, and take it onto the stage. It was time for Hattie to hide herself in the hat's secret pocket, just as Sammy had taught her.

"Here we go!" Hattie whispered.

She was just about to wriggle into the secret pocket when she stopped in surprise. What was *that*?

A fluffy gray tail was disappearing behind a pile of Sammy's boxes!

chapter three

Blinking hard, Hattie stared at the boxes. Was she seeing things? No, she really *had* seen a gray tail. Who could it belong to?

Hattie put her front paws on the edge of the top hat and peered out. Maybe she should go and take a look.

But I'll have to be very quick, she thought. *Sammy will be coming to get me soon.*

Hattie could see the tip of the gray tail sticking out from behind the boxes. But before she could do anything, it whisked out of sight again.

Hattie simply *had* to find out who that tail belonged to! With one leap, she jumped out of the hat and onto a nearby chair. Then, she jumped down onto the grass.

Henry was having a wonderful time sniffing around the boxes. There were all sorts of strange things inside them. Flowers made of feathers that tickled his

nose. Strings of silky flags. Big silver rings all joined together. Henry had never *seen* so many interesting things.

Hattie peered around the first pile of boxes. There was no one there. She would have to keep looking. As she hopped behind the boxes, Henry trotted out from the other side. He could hear the children clapping again. They sounded much closer now, just behind some big silver screens.

Henry was just about to run around the screens when he saw something very odd. There was a strange, round, black thing sitting on a table.

Henry climbed onto a chair to take a closer look. "What's this?" the kitten wondered out loud. He jumped onto the

table and, feeling very brave, went right
up to the strange object.

Henry stretched up on his back legs and
rested his front paws on the edge. Was
there anything inside? He leaned forward
as far as he could and peered over his
paws. It was very dark in there. If he
could just take a closer look . . .

He wriggled forward a bit
more — and suddenly felt
himself tumbling
downward. Henry had
lost his balance
and fallen in!

"Help!" Henry
mewed in alarm.
He scrambled to his
paws. The sides

around him were smooth and shiny, and it looked as if it was going to be tricky to get out. Henry looked down. What was *this*? There was some kind of pocket hidden in the bottom. Henry pulled the pocket open with one paw and wriggled inside. It was very soft and cozy.

"Now I'm really having an adventure!" he mewed proudly.

"And now," boomed a voice from outside, "I'm going to fetch my magic top hat!"

"Aha!" Henry mewed to himself. "So that's what this is. It's a hat. OH!" he exclaimed. The hat was being lifted high into the air — with him inside!

*   *   *

18

Hattie was still hopping around behind the boxes. She hadn't yet found out who owned that gray tail. *I'd better get back into the hat,* she thought. *It's almost time for my trick.*

She hopped out from behind the boxes and went over to the table. Then she came to a dead stop. The top hat was gone!

"Oh, no!" Hattie squeaked. She rushed to the side of the stage and peered around the screen. Sammy was standing in the middle of the stage, wearing his special magician's suit covered in silver stars. And he was holding the top hat in his hand! Everyone in the audience watched as he showed them the hat.

"Can you see anything in there?" asked

Sammy, tipping the hat so that they could look inside.

"No!" shouted all the children.

Hattie knew that normally it looked as if the hat was empty, because she was hiding in the secret pocket. *Oh dear*, she thought. *There really* isn't *anything in there this time — but Sammy doesn't know that!*

Sammy put the hat on a little table beside him. He tapped it with his magician's wand and put his hand inside. This was when he would usually lift Hattie out of the secret pocket. Hattie held her breath. What would Sammy do when he realized she wasn't in the hat?

Then Hattie stared in amazement. Sammy had lifted out a little gray-and-white kitten!

Henry was very confused. He had been ready to crawl out and see what was happening, when someone had reached into the secret pocket and gently pulled him out. Blinking in the bright lights, the kitten could see rows and rows of people staring at him. They were cheering and clapping loudly.

"Look, it's Henry!" shouted a voice that the kitten knew very well. It was Jamie. "Mom, what's Henry doing in the magician's hat?"

That's what Hattie wanted to know, too! The rabbit couldn't believe her eyes. Now she knew who that gray tail belonged to. But what was a kitten doing in *her* top hat, taking her place in Sammy's trick?

Henry began to purr. He still wasn't sure what was happening, but everyone seemed to be very pleased with him. He looked up at the man who was holding him. He was staring down at Henry with a puzzled smile.

"Who are *you*?" Henry mewed as the man put him down on the table. He rolled over to have his tummy tickled, and everyone clapped. Henry liked that!

Hattie watched miserably from the side of the stage. Her long white ears drooped. She couldn't help feeling jealous of Henry. The audience seemed to like that kitten even more than they liked her.

chapter four

"That was fun!" Henry purred.

The show was over, and Henry and Sammy were taking a bow.

Jamie climbed up onto the stage. "Henry, you were great!" he laughed.

"Is this *your* kitten?" asked Sammy. He was still holding Henry, who rubbed his furry cheek against Sammy's hand.

Jamie nodded. "Our cat had five kittens," he explained.

"He's adorable!" Sammy said. "And the audience loved him, too." He looked at

Henry thoughtfully. "Will you be looking for a new home for him?"

"Yes, we will," Jamie replied. He turned to his mom and whispered something to her. She nodded, and Jamie turned back to Sammy. "Would you like to keep him? Henry seems to like being a magician's cat."

Sammy smiled. "I would love to. Thank you very much," he said. "He'll make a great magic kitten!"

Hattie was still peering around the screen. Her ears drooped even more. "Why do you need a magic kitten, Sammy?" she snuffled sadly. "You have ME! And anyway, magicians always have rabbits. Whoever heard of a magician with a kitten?"

Just then, Sammy spotted Hattie at the side of the stage. "Hattie!" he called. "Why weren't you in the hat? Come and say hello to our new friend, Henry."

Hattie didn't want to say hello to the little kitten at all. But Sammy was waving to her, so she hopped slowly across the stage.

Sammy picked Hattie up and put her on the table. Then he put Henry down next to her. "Henry, meet Hattie," he laughed. "Hattie, meet Henry."

"Hello!" Henry purred. "I know what you are. You're a-a-a guinea pig. Or is it a hamster?"

"I'm a *rabbit*," Hattie squeaked angrily.

"Oh, yes," Henry mewed. "I got mixed up. Sorry." And he rubbed his fluffy head against Hattie's in a very friendly way. Hattie shuffled away from him, still feeling grumpy.

"I'm going to miss you, Henry," said Jamie, gently stroking the kitten. "Why don't you stop by our house on your way home, Mr. Spells? We'll give you Henry's toys and his food bowl and basket."

"Good idea," Sammy agreed.

Henry was pleased. Now he would be

able to say good-bye to his mom and sisters and tell them what a great new home he had. He was a magician's kitten now!

Jamie and Mrs. Watts left the tent, and Sammy took Henry and Hattie behind the screens.

"I'm just going to pack up my equipment," he told them. "Hattie, you don't mind sharing your basket with Henry, do you?"

Yes, I do, Hattie thought.

Sammy put Hattie into the basket first. She lolloped down to the other end and glared as Sammy popped Henry in, too.

"This is a nice basket," mewed Henry, gazing around with huge eyes.

Hattie didn't say anything. It looked like

Henry wanted to be friends, but she didn't want to be friends with *him*!

"It must be great being a magician's rabbit," Henry went on. "You must be very clever."

"Not really," Hattie snuffled. "Sammy taught me what to do."

"Well, *I* think you're very clever," Henry replied. Hattie couldn't help feeling pleased. "I'm sorry I got into the top hat instead of you," Henry added. "I fell in by mistake."

Hattie's nose twitched. It was very hard not to like the friendly little kitten. "That's OK," she squeaked.

"Tell me all about Sammy's tricks," Henry mewed eagerly.

Hattie enjoyed telling Henry all about

the magic show. She was still talking when Sammy finished packing up and drove them to the Wattses' house. Jamie and Mrs. Watts were waiting on the front steps.

Sammy opened the basket and took Henry out. Jamie cuddled Henry one last time, and then Sammy put the kitten on the grass so that he could say good-bye to his mom and sisters.

"Be a good boy, Henry," meowed his mom as Sammy picked Henry up again.

"Come back and visit us," Jamie said as they walked toward the van.

"We will," Sammy promised.

Hattie looked at Henry when Sammy put him back into the basket. The kitten's ears drooped, and he looked very sad.

"Are you OK?" Hattie asked kindly.

"I'm going to miss my mom," Henry whimpered as Sammy drove off. "And my sisters."

Hattie felt sorry for him. "But you always knew you would go to a new home one day," she reminded him.

Henry stared at Hattie with sad green eyes. "Can I snuggle up to you?" he asked. "Maybe I won't feel so lonely then."

"OK," replied Hattie.

The kitten curled up next to Hattie's soft white fur. He began to purr. Hattie realized that she might not mind having the kitten come to live with them. Henry was very friendly. And it would be nice to have someone to talk to.

"Henry, we're home," Hattie squeaked as the van pulled up outside a small white house.

Henry jumped up and peered out of the basket. He looked happier now. "It looks nice," he purred, staring at Sammy's house.

"I'll show you around," Hattie offered.

Sammy took Hattie and Henry into the house and let them out in the living room. Then he went outside to unpack the van.

"Hey, let's play chase," Henry mewed. He dashed into the hall and ran halfway up the stairs. Then he turned around to look for Hattie. "Come on!"

"OK," Hattie agreed. Before, when she got home from a show, Hattie would eat a couple of carrots and have a snooze. Things were going to be very different with Henry around!

Hattie lolloped up the stairs after Henry. The kitten waited for her, his green eyes full of mischief. When Hattie reached him, he raced off again to the top of the stairs. "Can't catch me!" he mewed.

Suddenly, Hattie thought of something. She went cold all over. What if Sammy decided he didn't want a kitten *and* a rabbit? What if Henry took her place in the show?

"What's in here?" Henry asked, peering into one of the upstairs rooms.

"That's where Sammy keeps all his tricks," replied Hattie.

"Let's go and see!" Henry mewed excitedly.

He trotted into the room, and Hattie followed. She was still feeling worried. She liked Henry, but if Sammy wanted a magician's kitten *instead* of a rabbit, what would she do then? Would she have to go and live somewhere else? She wanted to stay with Sammy!

"Wow!" Henry stared at all the shelves filled with tricks. There were silver rings, packs of giant playing cards, big silk handkerchiefs, and lots of different-sized boxes. He sniffed at a box that had a sparkly purple pattern on the outside. The lid was slightly open.

"What's in here?" he asked.

Hattie's nose twitched. She knew the box was full of purple glitter. A mischievous idea popped into her head If Henry spilled the glitter on the floor, then Sammy would be mad at him. And maybe he'd think that Henry was too clumsy to be in the show.

Hattie wiggled her ears and turned to Henry. "Why don't you take a look?" she suggested.

"OK," Henry agreed cheerfully.

Chapter five

Hattie watched as Henry put his front paws on the edge of the box. It tipped right over, and a shower of purple glitter flew everywhere. It went all over Henry, too!

"Oh!" Henry gasped, shaking himself. "I'm all purple and sparkly!"

"You look really funny!" Hattie squeaked. She wondered if Henry was going to be mad at her. But the kitten didn't look angry at all.

"What a great joke!" he purred. "Do you want some purple sparkles?" He ran over to Hattie and rubbed his glittery head against hers.

Hattie started to feel sorry. Henry was such fun. Maybe she shouldn't have tried to get him into trouble.

Just then, there were footsteps on the

stairs. Sammy came in, carrying a pile of boxes. He stopped when he saw the glitter all over the floor. "What have you two been up to?" he asked with a frown. Then he spotted Henry, and his eyes grew very wide. "Henry! Did you spill all that glitter?"

"Sorry," Henry mewed, bouncing over to Sammy. "I didn't mean to."

Sammy burst out laughing. "You little troublemaker!" he said. He picked up Henry and started dusting the glitter from his fur.

Hattie watched as Sammy cleaned the kitten. Henry hadn't gotten into trouble after all. Hattie was glad. She was beginning to like Henry a lot. She just hoped he wasn't going to take her place in the show.

* * *

"I can't wait to do another magic show with Sammy today!" Henry purred the following afternoon. "I'm really excited. Are you excited, Hattie?"

"Oh, yes," Hattie replied rather glumly.

Sammy was packing his magic equipment into the van, getting ready for a little girl's birthday party. Hattie and Henry were already in their baskets waiting for him. Sammy had bought Henry his own traveling basket that morning, so he didn't have to share Hattie's. But they could talk to each other through the wire doors.

"I wonder what tricks we'll be doing today," Henry went on. "I hope I can go in the top hat again!"

That's what I'm worried about, Hattie thought. Popping out of the top hat was her favorite trick. Was Sammy going to leave her out of the show from now on?

"Here we go, folks," said Sammy, climbing into the van.

They set off. A few minutes later, Sammy stopped the van outside a row of stores.

"Are we there?" Henry mewed, peering out of his basket.

"No," Hattie squeaked. "This is Merlin's Marvelous Magic Shop. Sammy buys all his magic tricks here."

Henry stared at the shop. *Merlin's Marvelous Magic Shop* was written in big gold letters on a bright blue sign above the door.

Sammy picked up the two baskets. "We're going to buy a new trick today," he told Hattie and Henry.

"Great!" Henry mewed happily.

Hattie didn't say anything. Was the new trick for *her*, or was it for Henry? As they went into the shop, Hattie saw that Sammy had the top hat tucked under his arm. She wondered why. Was the top hat going to be part of the new trick?

Henry looked eagerly around the shop. It was a bit like Sammy's magic room at home, but there were even more tricks here! Henry wished he could get out of the basket and explore.

"Hello, Mr. Merlin," Sammy said to the shop owner, who was standing behind the counter. He was a short, round man with a fluffy white beard.

"Hello, Sammy," said Mr. Merlin. "Have you come to see that magic box?"

Sammy nodded. Hattie and Henry watched as Mr. Merlin took down a red-and-gold box from one of the shelves. *The box is beautiful*, Hattie thought, twitching her nose with excitement. It was covered in sparkly red-and-gold glitter. And, when Sammy opened it, Hattie saw that it was lined with red velvet.

Sammy put the top hat down on the floor. Then he opened Hattie's basket, lifted her out, and popped her into the box. Hattie was thrilled. So this new trick *was* for her, after all! The box was lovely.

There was much more room than in the top hat, and the velvet was soft under her paws.

"Now it's Henry's turn," said Sammy, putting Hattie back in her basket.

"Oh, goody!" Henry mewed happily as Sammy lifted him into the magic box.

Hattie's ears drooped. It looked like Sammy hadn't decided whether the trick was for Henry or for her. Hattie turned around angrily, bumping against the door of her basket.

The door swung open!

Hattie jumped back, surprised. Sammy hadn't closed the door properly. She peered out. She could see Sammy's top hat sitting on the floor. Suddenly, Hattie had a great idea. If she jumped into the top hat right now, she'd be ready to do the trick when they got to the party! And if she did it really well, then maybe Sammy would let her have the sparkly box instead of Henry.

The rabbit pushed the door open a little wider with her nose and hopped out. Sammy and Mr. Merlin were still looking at Henry in the magic box. Hattie jumped quickly into the top hat and snuggled down in the secret pocket.

"Time to go," Hattie heard Sammy say. "That's right, Henry. Get back into your basket."

Hattie felt the top hat being lifted into the air — but then it was put down again. "I'll take the box now, Mr. Merlin," Sammy said.

"And I'll have this hat cleaned and mended by Thursday," said Mr. Merlin. "Bye, Sammy."

Hattie felt puzzled. She could hear Sammy walking away. But the hat stayed where it was. She stood up on her back

legs and peered out. She was very high up. Sammy was leaving the shop with the two baskets and the new magic box! Hattie's heart began to race with fear. Sammy was carrying too much to notice that she wasn't in the basket. And her hat had been put on a high shelf at the back of the shop. Sammy had left the hat to be mended — with Hattie inside it!

Hattie was very frightened. She didn't know how she was going to get down. And Sammy and Henry had gone off to the party!

chapter six

"Wasn't the box beautiful, Hattie?" Henry called across to the other basket as Sammy hurried out of the shop with his arms full.

There was no reply. *Maybe Hattie is having a little nap*, Henry thought. He was too excited to sleep!

"We'd better hurry," said Sammy. "We don't want to be late for the party." He put the two baskets on the seat and jumped into the van. He quickly started the engine and drove off.

Henry glanced over at Hattie's basket.

He could see right inside it now, through the wire door. He blinked his big green eyes. Hattie wasn't there!

Quickly, Henry jumped to his paws and mewed as loudly as he could, "SAMMY! SAMMY! STOP THE VAN! HATTIE'S NOT HERE!"

"What's the matter, Henry?" Sammy said as he stopped at a red light.

"HATTIE'S NOT HERE! LOOK!" Henry was starting to panic.

Sammy looked down at him and noticed the empty basket. "Oh, no! Where's Hattie?"

"I don't know," Henry mewed anxiously.

"She must have gotten out of the basket," said Sammy. "Quick, we have to find her." He turned the car around and drove back to the shop. When they arrived, he picked up Henry's basket and dashed into the shop. Mr. Merlin looked very surprised to see them again.

"Hattie's not in her basket," Sammy explained. "I think she might be somewhere in the shop."

Mr. Merlin frowned. "I haven't seen her," he replied. "But let's take a look."

Henry watched as Sammy and Mr. Merlin started looking. "Please let me out!" he whimpered. "I want to look for Hattie, too."

Henry made such a fuss that Sammy let him out of the basket. "There you go, little kitten," he said. "See if you can find Hattie."

Henry ran around the shop, looking under tables and in boxes. Where was she? He stopped and sniffed the air. He could smell something familiar. It was Hattie!

"She's over here," Henry mewed, following the trail to the back of the shop. It led up to a shelf filled with lots of top hats just like Sammy's. Henry craned his neck and peered up. Hattie was in one of those hats — Henry was sure of it. But which one?

Sammy turned to Mr. Merlin. "Which hat is mine?" he asked.

"I'm not sure," replied the shopkeeper. "They've all got stickers underneath with names on them."

"It'll take too long to check them all," Henry mewed. "We'll be late for the party! *I'll* find Hattie."

He quickly jumped onto a chair and scrambled up a tall pile of boxes. They wobbled dangerously as he climbed. Henry held on tightly with his claws, and soon he was high enough to leap onto the shelf.

"What's that noise?" asked Sammy. He looked up and saw Henry on the shelf above him. "Henry! What are you doing up there?" he gasped.

"Maybe he thinks he knows which hat is yours," Mr. Merlin suggested.

The shelf was very narrow, and there wasn't much room. But Henry carefully picked his way along it, sniffing all the time. Then he stopped by one of the hats. The Hattie smell was really strong here. "Hattie!" he mewed loudly. "Are you in there?"

Hattie was hiding in the secret pocket, feeling scared and miserable. She had tried to be clever and make sure that Sammy used her for the top-hat trick. But now it looked like she was going to miss the party altogether! Then she heard a very familiar voice.

"Hattie! Where are you?"

Hattie wriggled out of the secret pocket and popped her head out of the hat.

"Henry! I'm so glad to see you," she squeaked.

"And I'm glad to see *you*," replied Henry, rubbing his head against Hattie's.

Hattie started to scramble out of the magic hat. Being up so high made her feel dizzy, and she wanted to get down. But as she was about to jump out, the hat began to tip forward over the edge of the shelf!

"Help!" Hattie squealed.

"Hattie!" Sammy gasped in surprise. He leaped onto a chair and grabbed the hat before it fell.

"I was *so* worried about you," said Sammy as he stroked her ears. "Great job, Henry!" He lifted them down from the shelf and gave them both a big cuddle. "We'd better get going or we'll be late."

"Thank you for finding me, Henry," snuffled Hattie as Sammy hurried out of the shop. "I think *you* should be the one who goes inside the magic box."

"No, I think *you* should," replied Henry. "You've been a magic rabbit for much longer."

"We'll have time to practice our new trick just once before we start the show," Sammy told them as he got into the van. "I think the audience is going to love it!"

It was the end of the show, and Sammy had saved the new trick for last.

"And now, let me show you my magic box," he said to the children in the audience. He picked up the red-and-gold box. "There's something *very* special inside!"

Sammy opened the box, and the children laughed as a furry gray head popped up. It was Henry! He purred loudly.

"What can you see?" Sammy asked.

"A kitten," all the children shouted.

"Are you sure?" asked Sammy. He closed the box. Inside, Hattie got ready to pop up out of her secret pocket. This wasn't a trick for her *or* Henry. It was for *both* of them! They each had a secret pocket so that they could take turns popping out.

Sammy tapped the box with his wand. Then he opened it again, and Hattie jumped up.

The audience gasped. "It's a white rabbit!" shouted the little girl whose birthday it was.

Sammy closed the box and took a bow.

Inside the box, Henry wriggled out of his secret pocket and snuggled up to Hattie. "Isn't this a great trick, Hattie?" he purred.

"Yes! And best of all, it's a trick that we can do together!" squeaked Hattie.

"It's nice to be best friends, isn't it?" Henry mewed.

"Oh, yes," Hattie snuffled happily. "It's *magic*!"